In The Morning

by Virginia Mueller
illustrated by Diane Jaquith

HOUGHTON MIFFLIN COMPANY   BOSTON
Atlanta   Dallas   Geneva, Illinois   Palo Alto   Princeton   Toronto

One night, Rooster was talking
to Owl.

"Look," said Rooster.
"Look at the pig and
the cat and the dog."

"Look at the baby and the mother and the father."

4

"They are all sleeping now.
But in the morning, they
all get up!"

"Do you know who gets
them up?" said Rooster.
"Who?" said Owl.

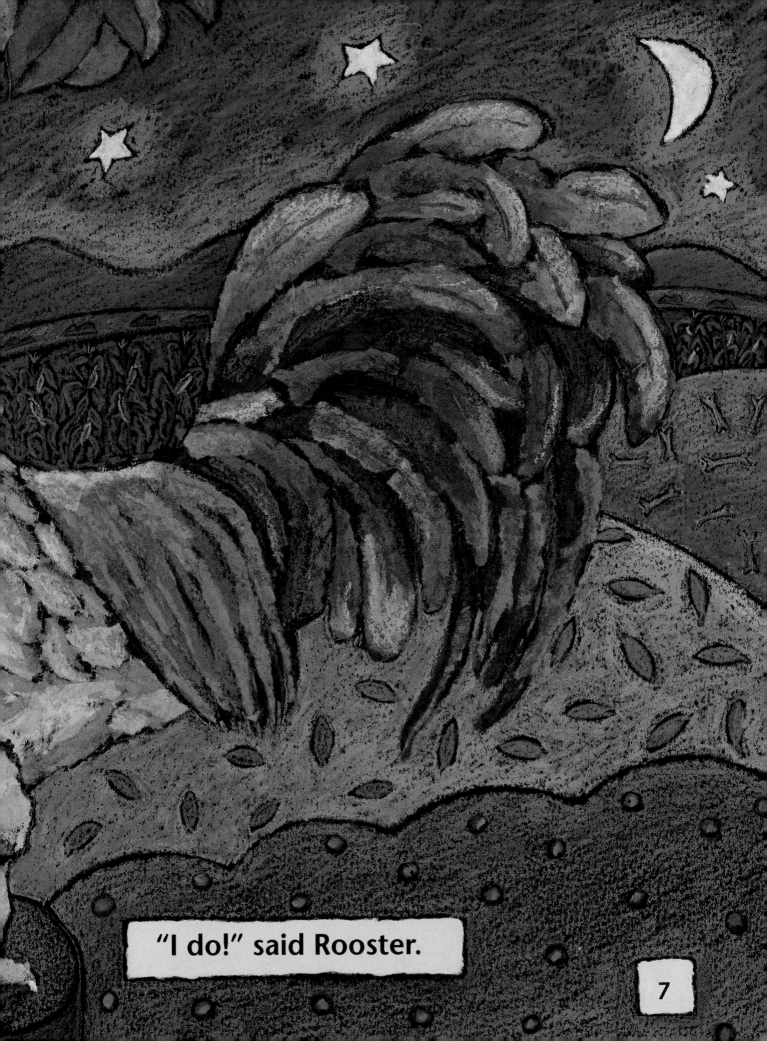

"I do!" said Rooster.

"In the morning," Rooster said,
"I get the pig up."

"The pig gets the cat up."

"The cat gets the dog up."

"The dog gets the baby up."

"The baby gets the mother up."

"The mother gets the father up."

"In the morning," Rooster said,
"They all get up, and I do it!"

"Who gets you up, Rooster?"
said Owl.

15

"I do!" said the sun.